# SHADOWED HEARTS

## Paranormal Love Stories

## Prof. Robert Stewart Ph.D

**V.F.Walker Publishing**

ISBN-13: 9798992090185


Cover design by: V.F. Walker Publishing
Library of Congress Control Number: 1991256
Printed in the United States of America

# FOREWORD

Shadowed Hearts is a captivating romance novel that transcends time and space, weaving a tapestry of love and connection through the realm of the paranormal. These enchanting tales explores the depths of intimacy and emotional bonds without the need for explicit content, making it a perfect choice for readers who cherish romance at its core. With its evocative storytelling and richly imagined characters, *Shadowed Hearts* invites you to embark upon a journey where love knows no boundaries, proving that true romance can flourish even in the most unexpected circumstances. Prepare to be swept away by love stories for the ages that will linger in your heart long after the last page is turned.

V.F. Walker Publishing

# SHADOWED

# HEARTS

### The Arrival

The sun dipped below the horizon, casting a deep orange glow over the ancient town of Eldenwood. Nestled between rolling hills and dense forests, the town had a reputation that thrived on myths and legends. Nora, a vibrant young woman with a passion for history, had arrived in Eldenwood to dig deeper into its storied past. Her enthusiasm for the supernatural made her excited to explore the long-forgotten tales that whispered through the cobblestone streets.

As she wandered through the marketplace, her fingers brushed against the cool, weathered stones of the buildings. The air was thick with the scent of earth and wood smoke, and the laughter of children echoed in the distance. However, a persistent sense of surveillance settled in the depths of her stomach. Nora brushed it aside, focusing instead on the quaint shops that adorned the main square.

An old wooden sign at the entrance of a peculiar antique store, bearing the words "Mystic Treasures," caught her attention. Curiosities lined the shelves inside, including dusty tomes, peculiar trinkets, and an assortment of oddities. At the back of the shop, the storekeeper, an elderly woman with a knowing smile, pointed Nora toward a collection of old maps and manuscripts.

"Careful, dear," the woman warned, her voice hushed. "Some stories should remain hidden."

Ignoring the warning, Nora spent hours sifting through the documents, intrigued by a map that hinted at a hidden castle in the nearby woods—Castle Nyx. A vampire lord, cursed to roam the shadows, awaited a fated love to break the spell, according to the legend. Nora's heart raced at the thought. Could it be mere myth, or was there a flicker of truth in these tales?

## The Legend of Castle Nyx

Determined to uncover the castle's secrets, Nora set out at dawn the following day, armed with the map, a backpack, and an insatiable curiosity. The journey through the woods was enchanting. Sunlight filtered through the trees, creating a dappled effect on the ground, while birds sang a melodic welcome.

As she traversed the overgrown path, Nora felt the pull of the legend draw her deeper into the forest. After hours of hiking, she stumbled upon a clearing that revealed the dilapidated structure of Castle Nyx, its towering spires reaching towards the sky, cloaked in ivy and mystery.

Upon entering the castle, the air inside was cool and

still. Dust danced in the beams of light that pierced through the broken windows. Nora felt a profound sense of both awe and sadness; this place once thrummed with life, now only echoes remained.

As she navigated through the grand hall, she came upon a vast library. The smell of aged parchment filled her senses, igniting her academic spirit. She traced her fingers along the spines of the forgotten books when suddenly, a chilling presence overwhelmed her.

"Who dares to disturb my sanctuary?" A deep voice whispered, leaving Nora frozen in place.

### Meeting the Vampire

Before her stood a man, tall and imposing, with raven-black hair cascading to his shoulders and piercing blue eyes that seemed to glow in the dim light of the library. He wore a sophisticated suit that transported Nora back in time. There was an air of sophistication about him, yet an undeniable darkness loomed in his presence.

"I... I'm sorry," Nora stammered, her heart racing. "I'm only here to explore."

"Explore?" he echoed, a hint of amusement dancing in his gaze. "You have ventured deep into a haunted sanctuary, little mortal."

Nora's curiosity bubbled over. "Haunted? Is that what they call you? A ghost?"

"Ghosts are mere shadows of what once was," he replied, stepping closer, his gaze never wavering. "I am Lucian, the last of the Nyx bloodline. It seems fate has delivered you to me."

"How do you know my name?" she whispered.

"I can sense the pull of destiny," Lucian said, a hint of longing in his voice. "You want to know the past, but do you fear these shadows?"

In that moment, Nora felt an inexplicable connection to Lucian, as if their souls recognized each other despite the chasm of time. "I fear only ignorance," she said, firming her resolve. "Tell me your story."

### The Curse

Lucian reluctantly sighed, compelled to share the

tale that entwined his existence. Lucian spoke of love lost centuries ago—his heart belonged to a woman named Isolde, whose beauty and spirit rivaled that of the stars. She had been a beacon in his dark world, but jealousy and betrayal had sealed their fates. A rival cursed Lucian, condemning him to roam the earth for eternity in search of the one who could break the curse with the kiss of true love.

"Only one who sees my heart will break the spell," Lucian finished, his eyes dark with sorrow and a glimmer of hope.

"A tragic tale indeed," Nora breathed, "but do you truly believe that your salvation rests upon a mortal?"

"I no longer hope," he replied somberly. "But your arrival stirs something within me."

Nora felt a shivering thrill at his words. Could she be the one to unravel centuries of darkness? The idea felt both exhilarating and terrifying.

### The connection deepens

As days turned into weeks, Nora found herself

returning to the castle, drawn into a world of history and mystery. Each visit deepened their connection. They spent hours discussing philosophy, art, and the intricacies of love, laughter spilling from their lips like music beneath the cold stone walls. Lucian revealed pieces of himself, scars of each lost love, and the weight of his eternal existence marked by solitude.

One evening, as dusk enveloped the castle in shades of blue, Nora found herself standing outside on the balcony. Lucian joined her, the cool breeze swirling around them, carrying with it the scent of blooming night flowers.

"Why do you come here, Nora?" He inquired softly, his gaze both penetrating and kind.

"I feel... alive here," she confessed, her heart racing. You give me the impression that magic still exists in this world.

He stepped closer, their breaths mingling in the night air. "And you bring back a sensation that is foreign to my existence. "But what would your heart say if it knew the truth?"

"Tell me," She pleaded, her voice barely audible.

He hesitated, emotions flickering in his eyes as he bowed his head. "My heart is tethered to darkness. To love me is to embrace the shadows within you."

Nora's heart ached, yet fear screamed within her to flee. But the yearning for connection drowned out that instinct. "We all have shadows," she said, trembling. "It's how we embrace them that matters."

<u>Love's Awakening</u>

As the moon grew full, illuminating the castle with beams of silver light, Nora stood at the threshold of her deepest desires. She had come to understand Lucian and the depths of his melancholy. She felt herself falling in love with him, but the shadow of his curse loomed over them.

One fateful night, as they shared a moment under the stars, Nora gathered her courage. "I want to break your curse, Lucian."

He recoiled, "Nora, you do not understand—there may be dire consequences. I am more than just a man; the darkness binds me.

"I choose you, Lucian," she declared, her eyes burning with determination. "Let me try."

"Do you understand what this means?" he asked, desperation creeping into his voice.

"I'm not afraid," she replied, reaching for his hand. "I want to know your heart."

### The First Kiss

Under the watchful gaze of the full moon, Nora leaned closer, their lips mere inches apart. Lucian hesitated, a flicker of uncertainty passing over his features. "Once touched by your lips, I may never return to the echoes of shadows."

"Then let it be so," Nora whispered, closing the distance.

As their lips met, a rush of energy surged through the castle. It was as if time itself froze around them, the air thick with magic and the sweet scent of night blooming flowers. Lucian's heart beat furiously within his chest—a promise of light breaking through an eternity of darkness.

But suddenly, the air crackled with a surge of dark energy. Nora pulled back, breathless and confused. Lucian staggered; his eyes wide with realization. "No, it cannot be."

## The Darkness Returns

Before their eyes, shadows began to swirl around Lucian, forming a vortex that pulled him away. "Nora!" he cried; anguish etched across his face. "Run! You must escape!"

"No! I won't leave you!" She shouted, reaching for him.

But the darkness was relentless, swallowing Lucian whole, and with an agonizing flash, he vanished into the abyss, leaving her in the stillness of the night.

Nora collapsed to the ground, choking on despair. Hatred coursed through her veins upon realizing that the curse remained unbroken, awaiting the perfect opportunity to manifest itself. She had to find him, to rescue him from the depths of darkness that threatened to consume them both.

## The Quest for Redemption

Determined, Nora delved into research, poring over the ancient texts in the castle library. She needed to uncover the real nature of Lucian's curse and find the key to his salvation. Day by day, relentless in her pursuit, she unearthed tales of powerful artifacts that could sever the grip of darkness—a blessed dagger steeped in moonlit magic.

With the blade in hand, Nora ventured back into the woods, following the whispers of Lucian's lingering essence. The forest, once welcoming, now pulsed with an unsettling energy. Shadows twisted around her, and faint echoes of Lucian's voice beckoned her deeper.

Finally, she reached a clearing where the veil between worlds seemed thin. There, she called out to him, her voice echoing through the night, "Lucian, I will not abandon you!"

## The Climactic Confrontation

With her heart pounding, Nora plunged the

dagger into the ground, invoking the ancient rites she had learned. The air thickened, shimmering with a celestial glow as she reached beyond the veil. She could feel Lucian's essence flickering like a candle in the darkness, pulling her closer.

"Remember, my heart," she whispered into the void, hoping he could hear her. "I choose you!"

Suddenly, a blinding light erupted, and a figure emerged from the shadows—a tortured version of Lucian, his eyes filled with pain. "Nora! You should not have come back!"

"I'll always come back for you!" she cried, lunging forward to grasp his hand.

In that moment, their hearts collided—the dagger amplified their bond, breaking through the chains of darkness that confined him. The shadows around Lucian wavered, slowly dissipating.

<u>Love Triumphant</u>

With courage and love intertwining, they surged together, drawing upon the power of their connection. As their hearts entwined, Lucian's true self emerged from the darkness, radiating with light. The spell was undone.

As the night faded into dawn, Lucian stood before Nora again—whole, unburdened, free. Tears of joy filled her eyes as their hands entwined, drawing them closer.

"Did we break the curse?" Lucian inquired; his expression filled with wonder.

"Together, we did," she replied, smiling through her tears. "Love conquers all."

### A New Beginning

With the shadows receding, the castle seemed to come alive once more, basking in sunlight they had long forgotten. The burdens of the past slipped away, enveloped in the warmth of newfound hope.

Soon after, the townsfolk began to notice the castle's transformation. The tales of the vampire lord became comical myths as Nora and Lucian told stories of unmatched love. They shared knowledge about history, tradition, and outer and inner myths, inciting a new yearning for exploration among the people of Eldenwood.

"One day, the world will know our tale," Lucian said, his gaze focused on Nora as they walked through the enchanted woods hand in hand.

"Don't you see? They already do," Nora replied, smiling as the sun dipped low on the horizon, casting a golden hue across the sky. "And it's just the beginning."

As they stepped forward, sunlit shadows danced, weaving together the threads of their past and future—two souls entwined in love's embrace, forever united against the darkness.

In the heart of Eldenwood, the tales of the castle became chronicles of love, and the echoes of their laughter mingled with the rustle of leaves, reminding the world that love was indeed the most powerful magic of all.

# WHISPERS IN THE SHADOWS

A young man named Ethan once lived in a small and unremarkable town, nestled between the mountains and the sea. He was an ordinary person who lived an extraordinary life in his own mind, filled with dreams of adventure and romance, ignited by the fantastical books he read during his evenings. Imagine a cozy living room, a warm amber light flickering from a table lamp, and the soft rustle of pages turning as Ethan immersed himself in tales of knights, serene beauty, and unfathomable mysteries. He often found solace in these stories, which allowed him to escape the mundane reality of his own world.

Ethan's life revolved around his bookstore, 'The Enchanted Pages,' a quaint little space packed with literary treasures. The air smelled of aged paper and coffee, a seductive combination that brought a sense of comfort to his heart. Consider walking into a small shop filled with towering shelves lined with vibrant book covers, delicate golden dust motes dancing in the sunbeams filtering through large windows. The light casts a glow over the fabric chairs where patrons linger, sipping coffee and losing themselves in stories.

One chilly autumn evening, as the sun dipped beneath the horizon, painting the sky in shades of orange and pink, Ethan was arranging books when an unusual customer walked in. She was breathtakingly beautiful (imagine a woman with raven-black hair cascading down her shoulders like a waterfall, her skin like porcelain, and eyes the color of the deepest emerald sea that sparkled with mischief). She introduced herself as Selene, and her voice seemed to wrap around him like a warm embrace.

As he offered to help her find a book, Ethan, entranced, stammered over his words. The chemistry between them was undeniable—an electric charge that sparked each time their hands brushed. They quickly discovered they both had a fondness for the uncanny and unusual, leading to a deep conversation that lasted well into the night.

After weeks of delightful encounters, they grew closer, sharing stories and laughs over cups of steaming coffee. Think of them lounging in the store's small café corner, surrounded by shelves brimming with adventure, their laughter echoing through the aisles as they exchanged playful banter. One fateful evening, Selene beckoned Ethan into her world of the supernatural, tempting him with secrets lying just beneath the surface of their ordinary lives.

"Ethan," she said, her voice low and conspiratorial,

"have you ever played with a Ouija board?" She leans closer, her emerald eyes gleaming with excitement and a hint of mischief.

Intrigued yet hesitant, Ethan soon found himself seated on the floor of Selene's dimly lit apartment, a flickering candle illuminating the air between them. The board lay before them, a wooden tableau marked with letters, numbers, and yes/no answers, seeming to pulse with energy. The atmosphere was electric, the air thick, as if the world had temporarily paused.

"Are you ready to communicate with the other side?" With a playful smile and a voice filled with mystery, she posed the question.

Ethan nodded, his heart racing from both excitement and trepidation. They laid their fingers on the planchette, the small triangular pointer that would direct their conversation.

"Spirits, are you here with us?" Selene asked softly, her voice barely above a whisper. Imagine her breath mingling with the scent of candle wax and a sweet, musky aroma filling the room—an essence that seemed uniquely her own.

For several moments, nothing happened. They exchanged glances, a shared giggle cutting through the tension as Ethan shifted uncomfortably. Suddenly, the planchette began to move, slowly but surely, gliding across the board.

"YES," it spelled out, and goosebumps prickled Ethan's arms.

"What's your name?" Selene pressed, curiosity igniting her features. The planchette danced eerily, revealing letters that formed a name: "M-A-R-I-A."

Unbeknownst to Ethan, he had unknowingly summoned a succubus—a spirit drawn to his youthful vitality and vibrant energy. Maria lingered between the veil of the living and the spectral, weaving in and out of realms as she began to entwine herself with Ethan's very essence. The candlelight flickered violently, throwing shadows across the room as Maria began to exert her influence.

Days turned into weeks, and the summoning of Maria breathed life into their relationship. Dreams haunted Ethan, strangely vivid and enticing, filled with alluring whispers and touches that felt both foreign and intimate. What he didn't realize was that Selene was not merely a charming girl; she was a gatekeeper to realms beyond, knowing fully well that Maria's presence would only complicate their lives.

Ethan's dreams evolved into lucid experiences. In these surreal dreamscapes, Maria felt like a forbidden lover, an ethereal figure who danced around him, enveloping him in warmth and longing. Imagine a lush garden under a shimmering full moon, where the air sparkles like diamond dust and Maria emerges from the mist, her figure fluid and enchanting. Their encounters in the dreamworld became increasingly intoxicating, leaving him breathless, thirsting for more.

However, as much as he adored Selene, Ethan found himself longing for more than just her warm presence. The boundaries of love tangled with unfathomable desire, and he began to split his affections between two worlds—the waking world and the realms of his dreams.

"Ethan, are you okay?" Selene questioned him one

evening when he seemed lost in thought, her voice pulling him back from the abyss. Her concern-filled eyes conveyed a depth of emotion that he struggled to comprehend.

"Yeah, of course," he replied, forcing a smile, but part of him felt as if he were drifting further away from her with each passing day.

The following night, he once again found himself on the Ouija board, this time asking questions of Maria, impatiently wondering what she wanted from him.

"Why do you haunt my dreams?" He whispered, his voice trembling with an inexplicable yearning.

"Because you called me," her haunting voice drifted through the air like a whispered secret. "You've awoken my spirit, dear Ethan. I feed and yearn for your life force."

Her words both terrified and thrilled him. The idea of a lover from beyond enchanted a part of Ethan, while a greater part recoiled in fear. "What do you want from me?"

"I want to be with you," Maria replied, her voice honeyed with promise.

It was then that Ethan realized the peril he faced —the allure of the unknown was intoxicating, but it came with a price. As he floated between dreams and reality, he felt his grip on Selene slipping.

Ethan made a choice. He had to confront Maria and sever the ties she had woven around his heart. The following night, under the light of a crescent moon, he returned to Selene.

"I can't keep doing this. I need to choose," he declared, his voice thick with emotion.

Selene's expression was resolute—understanding yet profoundly sad. "Ethan, your heart is torn. You must confront the spirit you called."

"What if I can't?" he whispered, shame flooding his cheeks.

"You must summon her again," Selene said softly. "Only then can you discover the truth."

Heart pounding, he returned to the board with

Selene beside him, fingers trembling as they placed them on the planchette. "Maria," he breathed, "come forth."

The air turned electric once more, shadows twisting as the candle flickered violently. "You summoned me?" Maria's voice resounded, echoing through their collective consciousness.

Breaking the surface of his fear, Ethan found strength in his convictions. "I choose reality. I choose Selene. I will no longer experience haunting.

A chilling laughter reverberated in the air, the temperature dropping as Maria's presence shifted. "What a foolish choice," she hissed, her voice dripping with malice. "You cannot escape what we share."

Yet, as the shadows closed in around Ethan, Selene held his hand tightly, grounding him. "You have the power," she whispered, a fierce determination igniting in her eyes. Together, they pushed back against the darkness, love blooming like a light in their bond.

"Maria, I release you," Ethan declared, heart steady

and voice unwavering. "I choose to live in the light, not be a prisoner of the dark."

The room fell silent, an unnatural stillness enfolding them. With a final shudder, the energy surged and then imploded, whisking Maria away from the realm of the living. Imagine the candlelight flickering wildly before settling, leaving a profound silence in the air—a calming embrace of peace that enveloped the room.

The realization of their freedom left Ethan and Selene breathless, their hearts racing. The bonds bore away into shadows, leaving room for the love that bloomed before them.

Days turned into weeks, and as Ethan worked alongside Selene at 'The Enchanted Pages,' the couple grew closer, their love uncomplicated and profound. Their laughter filled the bookstore, echoing down the aisles. (Visualize the fragrance of fresh coffee mingling with newly opened books as sunlight poured in, bathing them in warmth.)

Ethan realized that he found magic not in the haunting shadows of his dreams but in the tender love they had built together in reality.

The inexplicable connection to his past had faded, replaced by the promise of a life fulfilled by genuine companionship.

Though the whispers in the shadows lingered, reminding him of the temptation he had faced, those sounds faded to mere silence.

# BEAUTY AND THE BEAST

In the small, tucked-away town of Willow Creek, every night seemed draped in folklore and whispered tales. The town, nestled among towering pines and the expanse of the night sky, exuded an aura of mystery, particularly during the full moon. It was during one fateful full moon—when the silver glow of the moon illuminated the town—that an extraordinary love story began.

Elena Thompson had grown up in Willow Creek, a quaint town where everyone knew each other's names and secrets were as common as the morning fog. She was a spirited girl with chestnut hair that caught the sunlight like spun gold and eyes as bright as emeralds. At twenty-two, she had dreams as vast as the sky, from traveling the world to becoming a writer, yet she felt tethered to the familiar paths of her sleepy town.

One chilly autumn night, she ventured into the woods that bordered Willow Creek, chasing the sound of rustling leaves and the inviting scent of pine. The woods were a place of solace for Elena, as she found inspiration in nature's beauty while scribbling notes for her latest story. The trees towered majestically overhead, cloaked in shades of fiery red and burnt orange. The crunching of the leaves beneath her feet created a satisfying melody that instilled in her a sense of adventure.

As she wandered deeper into the woods, she stumbled into a clearing bathed in silvery moonlight. It was here that she first saw him. A figure emerged from the shadows, muscular and striking, with rugged features and an aura of wildness that both frightened and fascinated her. Derek, a werewolf with shaggy dark fur and fierce amber eyes glowing under the moonlight, was present.

Derek had lived in the woods surrounding Willow Creek for a century, an outcast of both the human and supernatural worlds. The curse that bound him to transformation during the full moon haunted him, endowing him with the strength of a wolf. The weight of loneliness weighed heavily on his heart, and each night of transformation only intensified his longing for connection. But the moment he laid eyes on Elena, something within him stirred—an unfamiliar feeling that whispered hope.

Elena felt an electric current course through the air as she looked into Derek's eyes, half expecting to run away in fear. Instead, she stood her ground, her heart racing. "Who are you?" she called out, curiosity overpowering her initial instinct to flee.

"I am Derek," he replied, his deep voice rumbling

like thunder in the still night. The moment their eyes locked, something unspoken passed between them—a bond, raw and profound. "I mean no harm. I simply haven't encountered anyone in these woods before.

Elena took a step closer, emboldened by her intrigue. "I come here often to write. This place makes me feel alive." The scent of earth and pine filled the air, a magical essence that only drew her closer to him. Derek's heart raced; never had he seen a human more captivating than this girl with the vibrant aura.

To his surprise, rather than running away, Elena asked, "What are you?" Despite her disbelief, she was genuinely fascinated by the man before her.

"A creature of the night," he replied, his gaze unwavering. "A protector of these woods, bound by the moon's curse."

As the weeks passed, Elena found herself returning to the clearing night after night, enticed by the magnetic pull she felt toward Derek. Under the silver moon, they shared their stories. Elena recounted tales of her dreams to write and explore the world, while Derek spoke of his long, lonely existence and the battles he fought—not just with external enemies but with the monster residing within. One evening, as the full moon illuminated the clearing, Elena mustered the courage to ask, "What if we could change our fates? Could we overcome the challenges we face?

Derek had never imagined a human could understand the complex nature of his existence. "I cannot change who I am," he replied, his voice filled with both sadness and resignation. "I run the risk of putting you in danger."

"Danger be damned," Elena declared passionately, her spirit unyielding. The air around them crackled with tension, with the distant call of an owl and the rustle of leaves in the night breeze punctuating the atmosphere. "I refuse to believe that love cannot conquer all!"

Her boldness surprised Derek. Derek had never experienced such intense attraction to anyone, let alone a human, and he remained cautious due to the potential danger his partner posed. But in the presence of Elena, he felt a stirring deep within that he hadn't thought possible—a flutter of hope that love could indeed transcend boundaries.

Their love blossomed, filled with stolen moments in the forest and shared dreams. However, Derek's transformation remained a looming shadow over their happiness. Each full moon brought uncertainty. On one particularly luminous night, as the moon rose high in the sky, Derek felt the rumble of change within him. He stood before Elena, his back to her, torn between the desperate desire to remain and the inevitable pull of the wolf within.

"Elena," he turned to her, his eyes filled with pain. "Tonight, I cannot control the beast. You need to leave."

"No!" she exclaimed, fear lacing her voice. "I won't abandon you! You're more than a creature to me. You're Derek!"

He shook his head, anguish etched on his face. "You deserve a life free from fear." You deserve a life free from fear, one without a monster lurking in the shadows."

With that, he transformed before her eyes into

a violent array of fur and muscles, reshaping him into the powerful werewolf. Even in his wolf form, his amber eyes held a flicker of the man she loved, tethered to her gaze. Panic coursed through her; she didn't know what to do.

In that moment of desperation, she reached out, tentatively placing her hand on his massive paw. "You are not just a monster, Derek! You are my love. Please don't throw away what we have."

He let out an unearthly roar, his primal instinct clashing with his determination to protect her. Yet, as she held his paw, something shifted. He felt the warmth of her love seep through the fur, grounding him.

In that critical moment, he realized that the beast did not define him completely. He could choose to embrace both sides of himself, human and wolf, and protect the woman he adored.

As the night wore on and the moon began to wane, Derek fought tooth and claw against the beast within, and as the first light of dawn broke, he stood before Elena as Derek once more—naked, vulnerable, yet filled with newfound strength.

Tears streamed down Elena's face as she took in the sight of him. "You did it! You fought him!"

"Not just for me," he said, pulling her into his embrace. "But for us. Love isn't merely about the absence of fear; it's about finding strength in vulnerability."

From that day forward, their love story became etched in the annals of Willow Creek. It was a tale of acceptance and courage, of a girl with dreams and a boy with secrets, defying the odds beneath the silver moon.

As seasons turned, Elena often wrote about their shared journey, crafting stories that celebrated the beauty of love transcending boundaries. Derek found solace in the knowledge that his love for Elena could coexist with his true nature, no longer shunned but embraced.

In the quiet moments, they would stand together in the clearing where their love story began, with the moon's glow illuminating a bond that would endure the passage of time. Together, they showed that even monsters could have kind hearts, and in that love, they found a world where anything was possible.

# ENTER THE INCUBUS

Once upon a time, in a little town nestled between rolling hills and a shimmering lake, there lived a young woman named Lila. Lilia was known for her long, flowing auburn hair that danced as she walked and bright green eyes that sparkled like emeralds in the sunlight. She worked as a gardener, spending her days planting vibrant flowers and nurturing the plants that filled the world with color. Lila was kind-hearted, gentle, and quietly adventurous, always dreaming of the possibilities that lay beyond the horizon.

Lila often felt a lingering emptiness in her heart, despite the many loves she received. In the evenings, as the sun dipped below the horizon, she would sit by the window, gazing at the stars with a longing in her soul. For something magical that seemed unattainable, she yearned. Little did she know that her life was about to change forever.

One crisp autumn night, as the leaves danced gracefully to the ground, Lila decided to stroll along the lake. The moon hung low in the sky, casting a silver glow upon the water that reflected the twinkling stars like a thousand diamonds scattered across its surface. As she walked along the shoreline, an unexplainable pull led her deeper into the woods that surrounded the lake. With each step, the air grew thick with an otherworldly energy, and the trees seemed to whisper secrets just beyond her hearing.

Suddenly, as Lila ventured deeper into the forest, she stumbled upon a small clearing. Fireflies flickered like tiny lanterns, enchanting the clearing with a soft, warm light. In the center stood an ancient tree, gnarled, and twisted, its branches stretching towards the heavens. Lila approached the tree, feeling drawn to its majestic presence. As she placed her hand upon the rough bark, an unexpected chill ran down her spine.

"Who dares to disturb my slumber?" a deep voice echoed through the clearing. The voice, rich and velvety, sent shivers of excitement and fear coursing through her. Startled, Lila stepped back, her heart racing. A figure emerged from behind the tree, leaving her breathless—a man with striking features, dark as the night, and eyes that glimmered like molten gold. His presence was intoxicating, and despite the warnings that tagged at the corners of her mind, she couldn't help but be entranced.

"I am Dorian," he said, a sly smile playing on his lips. His voice dripped with charm, though there was an underlying darkness that sent a thrill through her. "And I assure you, my intentions are not as wicked as they may seem."

Lila stood frozen, yet she sensed an undeniable connection to him, as if an invisible thread intertwined their destinies. She whispered, "What are you?"

"I am an Incubus," he replied, his smirk widening. The moonlight danced upon his tousled hair, giving him an ethereal glow, a striking contrast against the shadows that surrounded them. "A creature of the night, born of desires and dreams. I traverse the realms between fantasy and reality. But enough about me—a sweet soul like you deserves to know the beauty of the night."

Before she could protest, Dorian extended his hand toward her, and an irresistible energy pulsed between them. The forest around them faded, replaced by vibrant colors and an enchanting melody that enveloped her senses. Lila found herself swept into a world she had only dared to dream of, filled with celestial wonders and dazzling visions.

As the night unfolded, they danced among stars, whispered secrets into the wind, and laughed until her cheeks ached. (Dorian took her to places that defied logic—a garden of rainbow flowers that sparkled like jewels under the moonlight and a waterfall that flowed with shimmering silver water.) Lila felt alive in a way she had never experienced before, wrapped in the warmth of his laughter and the enchantment of the world he showed her.

Yet, as dawn began to break, a sudden heaviness settled in her heart. The vibrant colors around her turned to shades of gray as reality began to seep back into her consciousness. "Dorian, what will happen when the sun rises?" Lila asked, her voice trembling. He turned to her; his golden eyes filled with a depth of emotion. "When the sun rises, I will have to return to my realm. Although I can walk among the stars with you, I cannot stay in the light. He stepped closer, and the air crackled with an electric tension. She could feel his struggle between his desire for her and his limitations.

Tears brimmed in Lila's eyes as she realized the inevitable truth. "I don't want you to leave," she whispered. The sun's first rays began to emerge, casting a soft blush across the sky—a beautiful yet painful reminder of their fleeting time together.

"Neither do I," he responded, his voice barely audible. "But I can offer you a choice—a chance to be with me, but in my world. This may mean leaving everything you know behind."

Lila felt a whirlwind of emotions: fear, excitement, love, and uncertainty, all colliding within her. She looked around, taking in the beauty of her life—the garden she had created, the friends who loved her, and the simple joys of her town. Yet, standing before her was a love that felt as vast as the universe itself.

"I need time to think," she finally said, her heart aching with the weight of her decision. Dorian nodded, understanding the turmoil within her.

As the sun fully emerged, the vibrant world around them faded into mere memories, leaving Lila standing alone once more in the clearing. The ancient tree stood resolute, holding the echoes of their shared laughter. The weight of reality bore down upon her, and she returned home, her heart both heavy and hopeful.

Days turned into weeks as Lila tried to move on with her life. She often wandered to the lake, hoping to catch a glimpse of Dorian, yearning for the magic they had shared. But no matter how hard she tried, the emptiness in her heart only grew deeper. Each night, she would dream of Dorian, of the adventures they had and the promises whispered beneath the stars.

Finally, on a night when the moon was full and the air crackled with possibility, Lila knew she had to make a choice. The stars twinkled brightly above her, guiding her steps as she rushed toward the clearing, determination coursing through her veins. The stars twinkled brightly above her, guiding her steps as she rushed toward the clearing, determination coursing through her veins. When she arrived, the ancient tree stood waiting, and the clearing shimmered with anticipation as if it too awaited her decision.

"Dorian!" she called out into the night, her heart racing with hope. Moments later, he appeared, a vision of darkness and light, looking as stunning as ever.

"You came back," he said, his expression a mix of relief and delight. The moonlight kissed his skin, causing him to glow with an otherworldly beauty.

"I have made my choice," Lila declared, her voice steady. "I want to be with you, to embrace the magic of your world."

Dorian stepped closer; his eyes wide with emotion. "You truly desire this?" he asked, a flicker of disbelief dancing in his gaze.

"I've never been more certain of anything in my life," she replied. She felt the courage within her, the thrill of embracing the unknown.

Dorian swiftly grasped her hand, and a whirlwind of color and light enveloped them in an instant. The forest morphed around them, blooming into a surreal landscape unlike anything Lila had ever seen, pulsating with vibrant life and shimmering reality. The air smelled of sweet blooms and magic, and the stars felt closer than ever.

As they landed softly on a hilltop overlooking a fantastical kingdom, Lila gasped, her heart soaring. The sky was ablaze with colors, creatures of all shapes and sizes danced in the meadows, and castles gleamed in the distance.

"You are home now," Dorian said, his hand still clasping hers. He looked down at her, and she felt everything she had ever desired reflected in his gaze.

"Home," she whispered, realizing that she had finally found the place where she belonged.

From that day forward, Lila embraced her new life with Dorian. She learned about the magic of dreams, the art of desires, and how to weave her own essence into the fabric of this extraordinary world. Together they explored realms beyond imagination, celebrated the essence of life, and delved into the complexities of love.

In Dorian's arms, Lila discovered that true happiness came not from the absence of struggles but from the embrace of the journey they walked together. As the seasons changed and the years passed, their bond only grew stronger, with each moment weaving into the tapestry of their love story.

Together, they illuminated the night, leaving trails of magic wherever they roamed, crafting a love that fluttered like the delicate wings of dreams

—forever flowing, forever entwined. As they danced beneath the stars, Lila realized that every moment and every choice she had made had led her to this beautiful, mystical existence.

In a world that flourished with magic, Lila had not just found love; she had found her home within it.

# SHADOWS OF ENCHANTMENT

In the small town of Eldermoor, where willow trees swayed gently in the evening breeze and the moonlight danced upon the tranquil lake, life moved at a slower pace. The townsfolk held onto their traditions, gathered at the market to exchange goods, and shared stories beneath the starlit sky. However, a mysterious cloud hung over the northern cliffs, where legends whispered of a dark sorcerer, Loren, long shunned by the town, as the sun began to set, deepening the sky into hues of orange and purple.

Loren was a figure of intrigue and terror. People said that Loren, with his raven-black hair cascading down his back and eyes like molten gold, could command the shadows themselves. The townspeople spoke his name only in hushed tones, describing the eerie glow that emanated from his lair during the witching hour. He was rumored to possess dark magic, capable of bending the very fabric of reality to his will. To most, he was nothing more than a myth, but Amelia Hart, a curious and adventurous woman with a heart full of wonder, felt an insatiable pull toward the unknown.

One fateful evening, as the sun dipped behind the horizon, Amelia sat on the dock at Eldermoor Lake, her feet dangling above the water. She had heard the tales, yet they only fueled her determination to uncover the truth. She found herself captivated by the stories of Loren, drawn to the allure of something forbidden. Fireflies lit up the air around her like stars fallen from the sky, and as she watched them flicker, a thought lodged itself firmly in her mind: she would venture to the cliffs.

With her heart racing and the thrill of adventure coursing through her veins, Amelia set off toward the north cliffs as twilight enveloped the world around her. The path was overgrown with brambles and twisted roots, yet she pressed on, guided by an invisible force that thrummed through the air. As she climbed higher, the sounds of the town faded, replaced by the whispers of the wind and the soft rustling of leaves.

Upon reaching the edge of the cliffs, Amelia paused to catch her breath. The view before her was breathtaking. The moon hung low in the sky, casting silver beams across the lake, illuminating the water as if it were a mirror reflecting the stars. Yet her gaze was drawn to the shadowy figure standing on the precipice, bathed in moonlight, with a sense of ethereal grace.

It was him. The sorcerer. The tales hadn't done justice to his presence. Loren turned slowly, his golden eyes locking onto hers, sending a shiver down her spine. His expression was inscrutable, a mixture of amusement and caution, as though he had been expecting her.

"Why have you come here, brave little creature?" He asked, his voice deep and smooth, reverberating with an undercurrent of magic that seemed to swirl in the air between them.

Amelia's heart raced. "I wanted to know the truth," she replied, surprising herself with her own bravery. "Are you really a sorcerer?"

"Tell me, do you fear me?" He countered, stepping closer, the shadows around him seeming to dance with life. His proximity made her pulse quicken, a heady mixture of fear and fascination enveloping her.

"No," Amelia said, her voice steady despite her racing heart. "I find you... intriguing."

A brief silence fell between them, an electric tension sparking in the air. Loren's lips curled into a bemused smile. "Intrigue can be a dangerous thing, my dear. What you seek often comes at a cost."

Amelia's eyes flickered to the abyss behind him, then back to Loren. "I'm willing to learn," she said, her tone determined. "Teach me."

Loren regarded her thoughtfully, the shadows swirling around him like a living cloak. "Very well. However, bear in mind that the path I choose is not for the timid. Magic comes with consequences."

As they spoke, Amelia felt an undeniable connection spark between them, laced with an aura of mystery. She could sense the power emanating from him—a mixture of darkness and brilliance that both terrified and excited her. It was as if the very fabric of her being resonated with his presence.

Days turned into weeks, and Amelia found herself returning to the cliffs every evening, drawn to Loren like a moth to a flame. Their conversations flowed easily, filled with laughter and an unspoken understanding, each meeting deepening the bond that formed between them. Loren taught her about the elemental forces, the beauty of the night sky, and how magic intertwined with nature. He shared stories of his past—how he wielded enormous power in his youth, only to have it turned against him, leaving him isolated in the shadows.

Yet the more time they spent together; the more Amelia felt the weight of the darkness that surrounded him. Loren bore scars that ran deeper than the surface, wounds that seemed to shimmer with the remnants of betrayal and sorrow. There were nights when she caught glimpses of the anguish hidden behind his golden eyes, a flicker of vulnerability that contrasted starkly with his powerful demeanor.

One evening, as they stood together, the moon hanging high above them, Loren turned to her, a seriousness enveloping his features. "Amelia," he said, his voice low and deliberate. "You tread dangerously close to the edge. My world is one of shadows and pain. I cannot promise you safety."

She responded, her heart thumping like a drum inside her chest. "I want to understand you. I want to break down the walls you've built around yourself."

Loren's gaze softened, though uncertainty flickered across his features. "You must know that love can be the darkest magic, stronger than any spell I cast."

"Then let me choose," she urged, stepping closer, daring to bridge the divide between them. "Let me choose to see the darkness, to see you."

In that moment, the air hummed with an overwhelming intensity, and with a hesitant breath, Loren closed the distance. His hands found her face, his touch sending warmth cascading through her, a stark contrast to the chill of the night air. The world melted away, leaving only the two of them beneath the stars.

It was a kiss filled with longing, tenderness, and the aching weight of the shadows he carried. Amelia sensed a surge of enchantment enveloping them, as if the cosmos itself held its vitality in that singular pulse of intimacy. Yet as their lips brushed, Loren pulled away, anguish etched across his features.

"I cannot let you in completely," he said, as if the very thought pained him. "The darkness within me..." He hesitated, searching for the right words, but all he found were memories of despair that threatened to engulf him.

"Let me share that darkness with you," she implored, tears shimmering in her eyes. "I refuse to be afraid. If you let me, I can help you carry it."

But Loren shook his head, sorrow running deep in his golden gaze. "Amelia, you possess the ability to radiate brightness—don't tarnish it by selecting a path steeped in darkness." Leave now, while you can."

"I won't abandon you," she insisted, determination firm in her heart. "You've opened up to me in ways you never thought possible, and I refuse to turn away. Let me be your light."

In the ensuing silence, the weight of their emotions hung heavy in the air. Loren's heart waged a silent battle, fighting against the instinct to protect her from his world, even as he craved the warmth of her presence.

"Then join me," he finally whispered, a flicker of hope igniting within him as he reached for her hands. "Embrace the shadows. There is power in the darkness, just as there is in the light. Together, we can create a balance."

Amelia's breath hitched as the realization settled upon her: this was her choice. The journey before her would not be easy, but it was one she was willing to take, for the man standing before her was no longer a legend but a heart that needed healing. She nodded, her resolve stronger than ever.

And so, under the watching stars, their fates intertwined, Amelia and Loren embarked on a journey that would lead them through the darkest depths of magic and emotion. Each day brought new challenges as they explored both their powers and their souls. With every spell cast, they learned what it meant to trust one another and to close the gaps that had once seemed insurmountable.

Though shadows still lingered, they began to illuminate the dark corners of Loren's heart, revealing not just pain but the vestiges of hope buried deep within. Together, they danced on the precipice of light and darkness, discovering love that blossomed amidst the very shadows that once threatened to consume them.

In the end, it was not the power of the sorcerer nor the unyielding spirit of the woman that triumphed, but the unexpected alchemy of their bond—a love that transcended the darkness and embraced the light, weaving a tale that would be whispered in Eldermoor for generations to come. They discovered that every shadow and heart held magic and love.

# LOVE AMONG THE STARS

In a small town at the base of a mountain, life went on as usual. The townspeople woke up to the sound of chirping birds, the scent of freshly brewed coffee wafting from local cafes, and the pleasant hum of conversations filling the air. Among them was Emma, a curious twelve-year-old with an adventurous spirit. Emma had always dreamed of exploring the universe, her bedroom walls decorated with posters of galaxies, planets, and astronauts. The room was a vibrant mix of colors, adorned with glow-in-the-dark stars and colorful drawings of spaceships. Each corner whispered her desire for adventure.

One Friday evening, as the sun dipped behind the mountains, casting a golden hue over the town, Emma slipped out of her house, clutching her trusty telescope. She had promised herself that she would spend the night stargazing on the hilltop, hoping to catch a glimpse of the dazzling stars that twinkled like diamonds scattered across velvety black fabric. The hill, surrounded by tall, whispering pines and offering an expansive view of the universe that felt like an ocean of possibilities, was a sacred space for her.

As Emma set up her telescope, she felt a strange chill in the air—an electric current that sent shivers down her spine. She brushed it off as excitement, her imagination running wild as she gazed into the infinity above. Suddenly, a bright streak of light shot across the sky, illuminating everything in its path.

It was a shooting star, or so she thought. But as the light grew closer, it transformed into something extraordinary—a spaceship, unlike anything she had ever seen. The craft, a shimmering disc of silver, reflected the stars around it and exuded an otherworldly glow that made Emma's heart race with both fear and wonder.

The spaceship landed softly on the open expanse of the hilltop, and Emma, filled with both curiosity and trepidation, watched in awe as a hatch opened and outstepped a figure. The being was tall and slender, with skin that shimmered like the surface of a bubble in the sunlight, changing colors with each movement. Its eyes were large, luminous, and filled with an expression that was difficult to decipher—an amalgamation of curiosity and warmth. The colors danced across its skin like a living rainbow, and the sparkle in its eyes captured Emma, making her forget all about her fear.

"Hello," it said in a voice that resonated like a soft melody, echoing in Emma's mind. "I am Lyra from the planet Zenthia. I have traveled across galaxies to learn about your world and your people."

Emma could hardly breathe at the magnificence of this encounter. "I'm Emma," she managed to say, the thrill of the moment overshadowing her sense of disbelief. "What do you want to learn about us?"

Lyra stepped closer, its ethereal presence calming Emma's racing heart. "I seek connection and understanding. Your emotions, your experiences—these are treasures I wish to collect. The stars can feel lonely, and I believe love connects us all."

Emma felt an unusual warmth spread through her chest at the mention of love, a concept she had often pondered in her youthful naivety. She invited Lyra to sit and talk, sharing stories about her life in the small town, her family, her dreams of space travel, and her fondness for adventure. Each word vividly depicted her mother's laughter in the kitchen, her father's childhood stories, and her aspirations to become an astronaut.

In return, Lyra shared tales of Zenthia, a vibrant planet filled with enchanting landscapes, where the skies shimmered in every shade imaginable and flowers hummed melodies as they bloomed. "We communicate through feelings and thoughts, not just words," Lyra explained. "Love is the strongest force we know, surpassing even the distance of galaxies."

As the night grew darker, they created a bond that transcended the boundaries of their two worlds. Emma had never felt so understood or accepted. She learned that Lyra could sense her emotions, a gift that allowed them to communicate on a deeper level. The stars twinkled above them, providing a silent audience to this wondrous exchange between two beings from different worlds.

Days turned into weeks, and with each visit, they grew closer. Lyra's laughter echoed like music, and Emma found joy in the simplest of things—stargazing, sharing secrets, and exchanging stories of their dreams. They would sit on the hilltop for hours, Lyra teaching Emma how to feel the energy of the universe through the vibrations in the air, while Emma showed Lyra the warmth of friendship and love that human beings could share. Emma's heart brimmed with happiness, the world expanding with each adventure they embarked on together.

One fateful evening, as the stars glimmered overhead, Emma felt something shift in the atmosphere. Lyra could sense it too, and the playful banter that usually filled the air turned to a heavy silence. "What is it, Lyra?" Emma asked, her voice slightly trembling.

"I must return to Zenthia," Lyra said, its voice soft but firm. "The time has come for me to share the knowledge I have gained. My people await my return."

Tears welled up in Emma's eyes, her heart shattering at the thought of losing her friend, the one being that truly understood her. "But I don't want you to go!" she cried, feeling a wave of sadness wash over her. "You've become so important to me!"

Lyra stepped closer, wrapping its long, shimmering arms around Emma in a comforting embrace. "Distance cannot sever our bond, Emma. Love has no bounds, and as long as we share our memories and feelings, I will always be with you, no matter the galaxies between us."

With that, it was time for Lyra to depart. As the

spaceship rose into the sky, Emma watched it in awe, tears streaming down her cheeks. She felt a mixture of joy and sorrow, knowing that her love for Lyra would forever change her in unimaginable ways. The night sky seemed to dim, the stars holding their breaths in witness to this poignant farewell.

Weeks turned into months, but Emma never felt alone. She often revisited the hilltop, her heart aching yet hopeful. She poured her feelings into her journal, documenting the love that had blossomed between two worlds. Each page was filled with drawings of Lyra, illustrations of their adventures, and the moments they shared under the magnificent stars.

On one particularly starry night, while she was gazing at the sky, Emma suddenly felt a familiar energy, a vibration that sent shivers down her spine. Her heart raced as a silver light enveloped the hilltop. The spaceship materialized before her eyes, the same mesmerizing silver she had longed for. Out stepped Lyra, its presence radiant and warm, as if embracing the very essence of the universe.

"You came back!" Emma gasped, astonished and

overjoyed.

"Love knows no boundaries," Lyra replied, its voice echoing like a gentle breeze. "I carry you with me wherever I go. I have come to share all that I learned from my people about the power of love, and I want you to join me."

Emma's heart soared as she embraced Lyra, finally understanding the truth that defined their connection. Love had no limits, transcending time, distance, and even the cosmos itself. And with that, they knelt together on the hilltop, hand in hand, ready to explore not just the universe but the depths of their love.

From that night on, under the vast, twinkling canopy of stars, Emma became a traveler of the universe, her adventures accompanied by Lyra. Together, they learned that across galaxies, love was the ultimate force that bound them, forever leading them back to each other, no matter the distance that lay between. The cosmos stood witness to their journey, a testament to the extraordinary power of love forged in the heart of the universe and destined to last for eternity.

# THE CLOCKMAKER'S HEART

Nestled between the impenetrable mountains

and a glistening river in a small town, an old clock shop emanated the sound of ticking gears and the sweet smell of polished wood. [The shop was filled with intricate grandfather clocks, pocket watches adorned with delicate engravings, and wall clocks in whimsical shapes, each one chiming with a story of its own]. At the heart of this magical shop was Mr. Pendergast, an elderly clockmaker with twinkling blue eyes and a gentle smile that made all who entered feel welcomed.

One rainy afternoon, while storm clouds cloaked the sky, a young woman named Clara wandered into the shop, seeking refuge from the storm. [Clara was in her mid-twenties, with curly auburn hair that danced around her face and bright green eyes that hinted at her curiosity about the world.] She had heard tales of Mr. Pendergast's extraordinary clocks and was eager to see them for herself. As she stepped inside, the door creaked open, revealing a world filled with the soft golden light of the shop's many lamps, which illuminated the rows of clocks lining the wooden shelves.

"Welcome, my dear!" Mr. Pendergast greeted her warmly, wiping his hands on a cloth as he approached. "What brings you to my little haven on such a stormy day?"

Clara smiled softly, shivering slightly as she shrugged off her wet coat. "I'd heard about your wonderful clocks. People claim that some of your clocks possess a magical quality.

"Hah! Enchanted? Perhaps my clocks do have a bit of magic in them," he chuckled, his eyes sparkling with mischief. "But it's mostly just time and craftsmanship."

As Clara gazed around the shop, she noticed one clock that stood out from the rest—a tall, ornate grandfather clock standing isolated in a dimly lit corner. Intricate carvings of celestial bodies adorned it, while the shimmering glass face appeared to swirl with stars. She felt inexplicably drawn to it, as if it whispered secrets meant only for her.

"Ah, I see you've found my favorite piece," Mr. Pendergast said, noticing her gaze. "That clock is a special creation. Legend has it that its design not only tells time but also enables time travel.

Clara's heart raced at the thought. "Time travel? Is that even possible?"

"In theory, dear Clara, time is a river. Everyone flows in one direction, but what if you could navigate the stream in a small boat? This clock could potentially serve as a portal.

Skeptical yet intrigued, Clara stepped closer to the clock. "How does it work?"

Mr. Pendergast explained with a twinkle in his eye, "All you need is a strong desire and an exact moment in time you wish to return to. You set the hands of the clock accordingly. Just be careful—time is a delicate thing."

That evening, the storm continued to rage outside while Clara and Mr. Pendergast shared stories. She told him about her life, her dreams of becoming an artist, and her longing for adventurous experiences. The rain pattered against the windows, and the smell of wet earth drifted through the air, mixing with the scent of wood shavings and oil. In turn, he shared tales of his youth, of a love he had lost long ago, which lingered in his heart like dust in the air.

As the clock struck nine, its deep solemn chimes resonated through the shop. Clara felt a surge of boldness and asked, "Can I try the clock? Is it truly functional?

Mr. Pendergast regarded her with a knowing smile. "If your heart is true, then destiny may allow you to reach for those moments you desire."

With a mix of excitement and apprehension, Clara approached the clock. She closed her eyes and focused on a moment that had always tugged at her —a scene from a black-and-white photograph she had found in an old family album. It was her great-grandparents at a picnic, the sun shining and their laughter echoing through the air.

"1893," she murmured, setting the clock's hands to that year, the second hand ticking gently away.

To her amazement, when she opened her eyes again, the world around her had transformed. The vibrant meadow, where daisies swayed in a warm breeze and the sun poured down like golden honey, replaced the modern clock shop. Clara glanced around, her heart pounding with both exhilaration and disbelief.

In the distance, she spotted a figure—a handsome man with dark hair, wearing suspenders and a straw hat. As he approached, Clara's breath caught in her throat. He had deep brown eyes that sparkled with life and a heartwarming smile that melted her fears away.

"Hello there!" he called out, waving. "What brings you to this lovely picnic?"

Clara, overwhelmed, introduced herself. "I'm Clara. I must have taken a wrong turn."

"Well, you're just in time for a delightful lunch!" he said, extending his hand. "My name is Henry."

As they walked together, Clara felt an instant connection with Henry. They shared stories of their lives, and to her surprise, Clara found that every word flowed easily between them, as if they had known each other forever. [Laughter filled the air as they played old-fashioned games, shadows dancing beneath the sun's warm embrace.]

For what felt like hours, they laughed and shared their dreams. Clara learned that Henry was an aspiring writer who longed to capture the beauty of the world in words. They discussed everything from art to adventure, and Clara felt a longing bloom in her heart—a feeling of belonging she had never experienced before.

But as the sun dipped low in the sky, casting long shadows across the meadow, Clara's heart sank. She realized she had to return to her time. Leaving Henry would mean losing the connection they had built.

Seated on a checkered blanket, Henry looked at her, his gaze serious yet kind. "You look troubled, Clara. Is something wrong?"

"I... I have to go," she whispered, her voice barely audible over the rustling grass. "I don't belong here."

"Then stay," he said softly. "We could create a life together. You can write, and I could paint. We could be part of something beautiful."

Tears welled in Clara's eyes. "I wish I could, but I

have a life waiting for me."

As the final rays of sunlight faded, Clara took a deep breath, knowing this would be the hardest decision of her life. "I can't. I'm sorry, Henry. I didn't expect to meet someone like you, and now it's tearing me apart to leave."

Henry reached for her hand, his grip warm and reassuring. "Wherever you go, carry a piece of this moment with you. If there's one thing I've learned, it's that love is timeless."

With those words echoing in her heart, Clara grasped the hope of returning to him one day. In that instant, she knew she would find a way to preserve their memory. [As the first stars flickered into view, Clara closed her eyes, picturing the clock's hands as the porcelain ticked away].

When she unlocked them, Clara found herself back in the clock shop, her heart pounding. Mr. Pendergast was pouring over the clock as if he had known she would return.

"How was your journey?" he asked, his eyes gleaming with curiosity.

She replied, "Magical," with a slight tremor in her voice. "I met someone—someone who changed everything."

"That's the beauty of time travel, isn't it?" he said with a gentle smile. "Even brief moments can shape our hearts in ways we never imagined."

Clara nodded, grateful for the experience. But her newfound courage and love for Henry drove her to ask, "Can I go back again? Can I see him once more?"

"Time is a delicate dance, my dear. Mr. Pendergast warned, "If your heart's set on it, you must be willing to risk everything to achieve that connection."

"I understand," Clara replied, determination seeping into her voice. "I must try."

The clock chimed again, and she set the hands, her heart racing in the rhythm of hope. She felt the familiar pull—a gentle tug at her consciousness. With a fluttering heartbeat filled with anticipation and longing, Clara closed her eyes for the second time, ready to brave whatever lay ahead in the name of love.

As the clock ticked away, Clara realized she wasn't just chasing time but also a love that had already captured her heart—a love that could blossom at any age, at any moment, eagerly awaiting another embrace. With every tick, she felt the thread of destiny bind them together, intertwining their fates like the delicate gears of a clock, forever echoing through time.

# AWAKENING OF THE HEART

Once upon a modern time, in a bustling city filled with the sounds of honking cars and chattering crowds, there was a massive museum known as the Archaeological Wonders Museum (the building stood tall, its stone façade gleaming under the sun, like a giant preserving history within its walls).

Inside, the museum carefully displayed artifacts from centuries past behind glass cases, captivating every visitor who walked through its marble halls.

One fateful night, a powerful storm rolled over the city (thunder boomed, rain pelted the streets like a wild drumbeat, and the flickering lights danced ominously). The museum, usually quiet and serene, was filled with the echoes of nature's fury. The storm raged on, but deep within the museum's exhibits lay an ancient secret. Four thousand years had waited for the awakening of this ancient secret.

A mummy named Khepri rested in a darkened corner of the museum, behind a heavy glass case, his linen wrappings stained with age and his face serene, as if he slept in a peaceful dream. Khepri was an Egyptian priest who had lived during a glorious time in the Nile Valley. Treasures buried him, each symbolizing his life, his service to the gods, and his promise to awaken when the time was right.

As the storm raged on, a bolt of lightning struck the museum, lighting it up with a blinding flash (the power surged and alarms blared, scattering visitors into a frenzy). During that chaotic moment, energy surged into Khepri's tomb, gradually breaking the ancient spell that had kept him in slumber for millennia.

Khepri's eyes fluttered open for the first time since his burial. He took a moment to adjust to the strange, bright lights around him and the sounds of distant sirens and panicked voices (his heart raced as he sat up, the linen wrapping crinkling and rustling as though it had a life of its own). He felt an unfamiliar sensation stirring in his chest; it was fear, excitement, and curiosity all tangled into one.

He stood up, his legs stiff from centuries of stillness, and stepped out of the glass case (he marveled at the room around him, filled with strange machines and figures that looked nothing like the hieroglyphs he had known). The world outside was unlike anything he had ever imagined.

The large ceiling above him reflected stars of artificial light, and the air was cool and electric. Khepri walked cautiously, each step echoing against marble floors. He remained hidden in the shadows, still trying to process his awakening and the lingering memories of a life long ago.

Meanwhile, a young woman named Lily worked as a night security guard at the museum (she was tall, with dark curls cascading around her shoulders and bright, curious green eyes). Lily had always been fascinated by ancient civilizations, often losing herself in books about Egyptian mythology during her breaks. As she patrolled the exhibits that night, she felt a strange presence in the air—a mixture of energy and history blending together.

As Lily approached Khepri's exhibit, she noticed something odd. The glass case was ajar, the mummy missing from its resting place. Panic filled her heart (her mind raced, wondering if her imagination was playing tricks or if someone had been foolish enough to touch the sacred artifact). She rounded the corner and paused in shock as she saw Khepri standing there, his ancient face now imbued with a mixture of wonder and confusion.

"Who are you?" Khepri's voice resonated, smooth and rich with authority yet edged with vulnerability (it sent shivers down her spine). For a moment, Lily was too stunned to respond, caught in the gaze of his deep, piercing eyes.

"I—I'm Lily," she finally stammered, her voice trembling but filled with a strange excitement. "What happened to you? You... you came back to life!"

"I am Khepri," he replied, taking a hesitant step closer (he felt an inexplicable pull toward this curious woman). "I have lived in darkness for too long. The storm has awakened me, but I do not understand what I see. This land is unfamiliar."

Lily's heart raced as she studied his features—strong, noble, and strangely beautiful (the contrast between her modern attire and his ancient appearance created a moment that felt surreal, almost like a dream). "You're in a museum now. This is Chicago. It's the year 2023."

"Chicago?" Khepri echoed, his brow furrowing as if the name held weight. "You say many years have passed?"

"Yes, thousands. Your civilization was great, Khepri. You served the gods of the Nile—Ra, Osiris... You were a priest."

Khepri's heart surged at the mention of names that had once filled his life with purpose (memories flashed in his mind—grains of sand, the perfume of lotus flowers, and the sacred rituals performed with immense reverence). "It is a strange world that grows so far from the river."

Feeling an unexpected surge of courage, Lily took a step toward him. "It must be strange for you. I can help you. I can tell you about—"

A loud crash from behind cut her short. Drawn by the alarms, a group of security guards entered the room, their flashlights beaming and darting, illuminating Khepri in a way that made him look even more otherworldly.

Lily instinctively moved to shield Khepri from their view, her heart racing with fierce determination to protect this ancient being. "No, wait! Please, it's not what you think!"

"Step away from that thing!" one of the guards shouted, their eyes wide with disbelief.

Khepri turned to Lily, confusion etched on his

ancient face. "You cannot see me as I am." This time is not appropriate for my presence.

Lily looked at him. "But you shouldn't be afraid. You're part of history, part of the story of humanity."

At that moment, Khepri felt a stirring within him, something more profound than the bindings of time and space (an emotion flooded him, and he realized he didn't want to vanish back into the darkness of his tomb). He reached out, taking Lily's hand with immense gentleness, and the moment their skin touched, a spark ignited between them.

"Together we can find a way," he said, his voice steady now, a quiet strength resonating with every word.

Before the guards could react, Lily and Khepri dashed down the hall, their footsteps pounding in sync against the polished floors. They raced through the maze of exhibits, passing mummies, relics, and treasures, all while Khepri took in the astounding new world filled with colors, lights, and the hopeful rhythm of life (his heart raced, not merely from fear but with an unexpected joy).

They found a small exit door leading to a back alley (the storm had subsided, casting a calmness that enveloped them like a soft embrace). As they stepped outside, the cool air hit Khepri's face—so free, so alive.

Lily turned to him amidst the quiet night. "What do you want to do now?"

Khepri studied her, deeply aware of how his heart had quickly formed an unbreakable bond with this brave woman, the trust in her eyes making him feel more alive than he had in ages. "I want to learn. I want to understand this new world and the people within it."

With a determined smile, Lily replied, "Then we'll learn together."

As their journey began, they explored the city that never slept. Khepri marveled at things that glittered and beamed in the night: the neon signs, the skyscrapers that reached for the heavens, and the mesmerizing dance of technology that contrasted sharply with his earthly past (he felt as though he was reborn).

Day by day, Khepri absorbed knowledge like a sponge—learning about the pulse of life in modern society, the complexities of human emotions, and the wonders of love that transcended time. As he shared stories of ancient Egypt, Lily found herself captivated by not just his tales but also the kindness in his heart.

The bond between Khepri and Lily deepened. She felt the echoes of his ancient wisdom while he learned about the beauty and fragility of the world they lived in now (including the wondrous complexity of human connections). Underneath the digital stars of the city, their love blossomed into something magical and sublime.

But as weeks passed, Khepri knew the time had come to confront the reality of his existence. He could not remain in this world forever. Though he had tasted the sweetest nectar of love, the past always lingered in the shadows of his heart (like a whisper, urging him to return).

One evening, as they stood on the rooftop of a tall building watching the sunset paint the sky in hues of gold and crimson, Khepri turned to Lily, his heart heavy yet filled with a deep appreciation for her. "My destiny calls me back, Lily. I cannot stay in this world forever."

Tears welled in Lilly's eyes. "But Khepri, you belong here! We found each other."

"I must return to the sands of my homeland—the place where my spirit rests. But know this: you have awakened my heart from a slumber deeper than sleep. You are a part of me, always."

With a deep sigh, Lily realized the truth in Khepri's words. Their love was timeless, bound by moments, memories, and the powerful connection they had forged (despite their worlds being completely different).

In that moment, they shared a kiss that was electric and brimming with enduring love.

# THE FLAME
# OF DESIRE

A man named Ethan lived in the bustling heart of New York City, where the days hummed with the chatter of dreams and the nights painted with the glow of vibrant lights. [Ethan was in his early thirties, with tousled dark hair and a pair of sky-blue eyes that often gazed longingly out of his small apartment window. He was tall and had a lean build, but despite his outward appearance, his heart felt heavy with an unshakable sense of loneliness. He often buried himself in the books lining the walls of his apartment, seeking escape from the mundaneness of life, but the stories within failed to provide the warmth of companionship he so desperately craved.

Ethan worked as a graphic designer, his days filled with colors and designs, creating worlds that didn't exist but should have. Yet when he returned home each evening, the silence of his apartment loomed like an unwelcome guest. On one particularly rainy night, with gray clouds hanging low and the smell of wet pavement wafting through the air, Ethan decided to break his routine. He ventured out to a small café he had always passed but never entered. The café, painted in deep shades of burgundy and adorned with tiny string lights, exuded charm. Its wooden sign, slightly askew, read "Café Nocturne," and inside, the smell of freshly brewed coffee blended with the soft sound of jazz music that swept through the air like a gentle kiss.

As he entered, the doorbell chimed softly,

and the warmth enveloped him. He ordered his usual—an espresso—and found a corner table near a window. The café was a cozy refuge, filled with mismatched furniture and a collection of quirky artworks hanging askew on the walls. The low hum of conversation and the clinking of cups created a symphony of warmth that momentarily melted Ethan's solitude. As he sipped his drink, he noticed a group of friends laughing boisterously in the next corner, their joy contrasting sharply with his stillness.

That's when his gaze fell upon her—a woman sitting alone at a small table across the room. She was breathtakingly beautiful, with long, flowing black hair that cascaded over her shoulders like a waterfall of night. Her skin glowed with an ethereal light, and her green eyes sparkled with a mischief that seemed out of place in the dim café lighting. She wore a fitted red dress that clung to her curves perfectly, and every time she lifted her glass of wine to her lips, Ethan felt a strange pull towards her as if an invisible string connected them.

Ethan caught her eye, and for a fleeting moment, time seemed to stand still. She smiled—a slow, enchanting smile that sent a jolt of warmth through him. He felt a flush rise to his cheeks; his heart raced like he'd just sprinted a mile. To his surprise, she raised her glass in a toast, as if inviting him into her world. Without fully understanding why, he stood and walked towards her table, the sound of his footsteps muted by the soft ambiance around them.

"Is this seat taken?" Ethan asked, his voice steady despite the butterflies swarming in his stomach.

"No, please join me," she replied, her voice sultry and smooth like honey. "I'm Althea."

"Ethan," he introduced himself, sinking into the chair across from her. The moment their eyes met again, Ethan felt an electric connection, as if the universe had conspired to bring them together. Althea leaned forward slightly, her gaze piercing yet inviting, and he noticed a faint hint of mischief dancing in her expression.

"So, what brings you to this corner of the world on a rainy night?" she asked.

Ethan chuckled nervously. "I guess I was looking for something different, something to shake off the same old routine."

"Routine can be a killer, can't it?" Althea replied, swirling her wine thoughtfully. "You know, it's in the unexpected moments that we often find ourselves."

Her words resonated deep within him. They spoke for a while, their conversation flowing easily as if they were old friends catching up. Ethan found solace in her laughter, a melodic sound that drew people's attention. He learned that Althea was an artist too, a painter who often sought inspiration from the beauty of the night. With each word, he felt more captivated, as if she were slowly peeling back the layers of his loneliness, exposing the yearning he had buried for too long.

As the night wore on, their connection deepened, and the café's ambience dimmed with the passage of time. Ethan learned that Althea had a mysterious charm about her, a certain allure that made him uneasy yet exhilarated. She spoke of adventures in distant lands, of dreams painted under the stars, and tales that felt like whispers from another realm. It was intoxicating, as if she were weaving a spell that encircled him in warmth and light.

Finally, closing time rolled around, and reluctantly, they both stood to leave, a tangible tension lingering in the air, thick and sweet. "Can we meet again?" Ethan inquired, his voice brimming with hope.

"Tomorrow night, same time? I have some paintings I'd love to share with you," Althea replied, her eyes sparkling with mischief. Suddenly, the evening concluded with a promise that stirred his heart.

The city felt different as he walked home —brighter, full of possibilities, as if the very air charged with anticipation. The rain had ceased, and the moon hung gracefully in the night sky, casting a silvery glow. Ethan found himself smiling; the heaviness in his heart lifted for the first time in a long while. He thought about Althea and the way she had made him feel, as radiant as the moon itself.

The next night arrived all too quickly. As Ethan entered Café Nocturne, his heart fluttered at the sight of Althea waiting for him at the same table. She was even more beautiful than he remembered, her dress shimmering subtly under the café lights. With every step toward her, he felt the anticipation building—a mixture of excitement and an inexplicable fear of what he was uncovering.

"Ethan!" Althea called, her expression brightening as she waved him over. "I've been impatiently waiting."

They settled into their seats, and she quickly began showing him her paintings—each one more exquisite and captivating than the last. They depicted ethereal landscapes filled with swirling colors and fantastical creatures, each brushstroke telling a story that seemed to transcend reality.

"What inspires you?" Ethan asked, completely entranced.

"In the world of dreams," she said, her eyes twinkling with a secret. "My visions originate from a realm, and each brushstroke weaves a fragment of that realm into our reality."

"Sounds enchanting," Ethan replied, his heartbeat echoing in his ears.

"It is," she whispered, leaning closer, her breath warm and inviting. "But not everyone can see it."

Suddenly, despite the warmth and joy, a slight chill crept into Ethan's heart, and the air around them thickened as if a veil had drawn between the worlds. "What do you mean?"

Althea paused, her gaze earnest. "Not everyone understands or accepts what truly lies in the shadows. Certain creatures exist where dreams and reality collide.

A flicker of uncertainty ignited in Ethan. Her words danced along the periphery of his consciousness, hinting at something beyond the mundane. Before he could press further, she smiled again, brushing off the weight of her words. "Let's not dampen our evening with tales of shadows, shall we?"

As the weeks passed, they met nightly, exploring the depths of their hearts and dreams. It was a whirlwind romance, vibrant with laughter, stolen glances, and whispering secrets. [Ethan found solace in Althea, a spirit that lit his world aflame, illuminating the dark corners of his existence. Yet with each passing day, he felt an unshakeable bond growing, one he couldn't quite explain. Unseen threads connected their very souls.

But amid the laughter and shared dreams, moments of unease whispered like the haunting shadows in Althea's art. While he felt an inexplicable safety in her arms, shadows danced along the edges of his awareness.

One evening, as they strolled hand-in-hand through Central Park, the moon casting a pale glow on them, Ethan finally summoned the courage to confront the words she had once spoken. "Althea," he began, the cool breeze tousling his hair, "what did you mean about shadows? What lies between dreams and reality?"

Althea's expression shifted, a solemn veil settling over her. Her laughter faded, replaced by a thin line of concern etched on her brow. "Some truths are heavy, Ethan. I'm not just an artist; I'm a succubus —a being that draws energy from the dreams of mortals. You are my muse, and while our connection is real, it comes with a price."

Ethan's heart raced; he searched her eyes for any sign of deceit, but all he saw was honesty and vulnerability. "A succubus?" he echoed, his mind racing. The world around him blurred, the crickets chirping a chilling symphony that echoed in his ears. He felt as if he were standing on the precipice of a deep abyss, peering into the unknown.

"Yes," she affirmed, stepping closer, her hand still entwined with his. "But I am not here to harm you. You've brought light into my life, too. It's a dance of wants—the energy I take is filled with your longing, your dreams.

# THE TIDES OF LOVE

In a coastal village where the land kissed the sea, there lived a man named Samuel. He was a rugged fisherman with sun-kissed skin, tousled brown hair, and deep blue eyes that mirrored the ocean he loved to navigate. His days were filled with hauling nets and battling the waves, but each night, he returned to a quiet home that echoed with loneliness and longing. As the sun dipped below the horizon, painting the sky in shades of orange and pink, Samuel would often sit on the rocky shore, staring at the vastness of the sea, dreaming of love.

One fateful evening, a gentle breeze danced through the air, carrying with it salty whispers of the ocean's secrets. Samuel decided to take his boat out, letting the rhythmic lull of the waves soothe his restless heart. The water shimmered under the moonlight, creating a silver path that beckoned him further into the deep. With every stroke of the oars, he felt a connection to the sea, but a deeper desire echoed in his heart—the yearning for someone to share his life with.

As he drifted farther from the shore, the moon hung high above, casting a soft glow that illuminated the water like diamonds. Suddenly, the surface began to stir, and Samuel's breath caught in his throat as a figure emerged from the depths —a mermaid, enchanting and ethereal. Her long, flowing hair sparkled with droplets of sea foam, cascading over her glistening scales that shimmered in hues of deep green and blue. Her eyes, luminous like pearls, held a mysterious depth that captivated Samuel instantly.

"Who are you?" Samuel gasped, unable to take his eyes off her.

"I am Seraphina, guardian of these waters," she replied, her voice as melodic as a siren's song, wrapping around him like a warm embrace. "You called to me, did you not?"

Samuel shook his head, bewildered yet intrigued. "I'm just a lonely fisherman." "I never expected to see a mermaid."

A soft smile danced on Seraphina's lips. "The sea has heard your heart's wish. It brings me to you."

As night deepened, they spoke until the first hint of dawn painted the sky in soft pastels. Samuel shared stories of his life, his dreams, and his longing for love, while Seraphina spoke of her kingdom beneath the waves—a vibrant world filled with coral palaces, playful dolphins, and hidden treasures. Her voice was soothing, akin to the calming sound of waves crashing against the shore, and for the first time in ages, Samuel felt understood.

Over the following weeks, they met every

night at the same spot. Every time he witnessed her rising from the depths, his heart fluttered with joy. They learned about each other's worlds, navigating the chasm between land and sea with laughter and shared dreams. Seraphina showed Samuel the wonders of her underwater realm, taking him on imaginative journeys as she described the colorful schools of fish that swam through the reefs and the luminescent jellyfish that floated gracefully in the dark.

Samuel, in turn, shared the beauty of the land —stories of the sunsets that melted into the ocean, the sweet scent of the flowers that blossomed during spring, and the warmth of human connections, evoking vivid dreams of a life yet to be lived together. As they spent countless nights together, their bond deepened with every shared secret and stolen glance.

But as the days turned into weeks, Samuel grew aware of an unspoken challenge. (He would often look into Seraphina's eyes, seeing both the depth of the ocean and the heart of a woman who desired more than her watery realm could offer.) The stark reality was that he belonged to the land and she to the sea. They were deeply in love, but their differences kept them apart.

One particularly enchanting evening, Seraphina surfaced, illuminating the water with her iridescent glow. "Samuel," she began cautiously, "I feel our hearts intertwining like the currents of the ocean, but we cannot ignore the truth. The land meant you, and the sea bound me.

Samuel felt a pang of sorrow at her words. "I do not want to lose you, Seraphina. My heart has never known such joy until you came into my life."

Seraphina approached him, her gaze steady. "Love is a powerful force. It can transcend barriers, but it cannot change our world. I love you too, Samuel. But what we have is precious, even if it cannot be forever."

In the days that followed, Samuel grappled with his emotions. Every sunrise made the shadows of his heart loom larger. He watched the waves crash against the rocks and longed for the enchantment of Seraphina's presence. As he sat on the shore, contemplating their unattainable love, an idea dawned on him—perhaps love could triumph over all.

That night, he called out to Seraphina, determined to make a choice. "I will not lose you, not without a fight. I will dive into the depths of the sea and find a way to be with you."

"Samuel, no!" Seraphina exclaimed, panic rising in her voice. "The sea is dangerous for those who do not belong to it. You cannot change who you are or what you were born to be."

"Perhaps not," he replied with resolve. "But I will find a way to bridge the gap between our worlds. Love must be more powerful than any barrier."

Time passed quickly as Samuel immersed himself in his quest. He researched ancient tales of transformation and sought the counsel of the village elders. The village elders, their faces adorned with years of wisdom, spoke with the weight of lost loves and long-forgotten stories. After many sleepless nights, he discovered a legend about a powerful sea witch who could grant mortals the gift of the sea, but her spells came with a price: to live in the depths, one would have to surrender their old life entirely.

With a heavy heart, Samuel set out to find the sea witch. The journey was treacherous, filled with raging tides and sprawling caves, but his love for Seraphina fueled his determination. As he swam deeper, the air grew cold and salty, and the light from above faded into darkness. Finally, he found the witch, cloaked in shadows, amidst swirling sea creatures and ancient treasures.

"What is it you seek, mortal?" The witch rasped, her eyes glinting like sharp blades.

"I wish to become one with the sea, to be with my love, Seraphina," he declared boldly.

The witch contemplated his request, her gaze piercing through him. "To become a creature of the sea, you must give up everything you know. Are you willing to pay the price?"

"I am," Samuel replied without hesitation.

"Very well. You will change when the moon is full, but once you accept your gift, you cannot go back.

With a nod, Samuel submerged himself

back into the ocean, feeling the currents wrap around him as though welcoming him home. As the night descended, Samuel felt a tingling sensation throughout his entire being. He closed his eyes and surrendered to the magic of the transformation. When he opened his eyes, he realized he had grown a shimmering tail that radiated every color of coral.

He swam with newfound strength, navigating the depths with ease until he found Seraphina near their usual meeting place. When she saw him, her eyes widened in astonishment. "Samuel! You did it! You became one with the sea!"

"I did it for you, Seraphina," he replied, feeling a surge of joy as he swam gracefully alongside her. "Now we can explore both our worlds together."

They spent the night weaving through coral reefs and playing alongside dolphins, reveling in their love that transcended the boundaries once placed upon them. The vibrant colors of the underwater world engulfed them, making every moment feel like a realization of their dreams.

As the days turned into weeks, Samuel embraced his new life as a merman. He and Seraphina ruled the underwater kingdom side by side, preserving the wonders of the sea and teaching one another the beauty of their former lives. (They held hands as they swam, their souls intertwined, creating a love story that became legendary—a tale of two worlds coming together, forged by a love that was meant to last through the ages.)

Yet, as beautifully as their union blossomed, a lingering thought danced in Samuel's heart. The connection he had with the land—the ongoing sounds of laughter, the colors of bloom in spring, and the warmth of the sun on his skin—was a world he had left behind. One evening, seated on a coral throne that glimmered in the light of shimmering fish, he turned to Seraphina. "My love, while I have embraced this life with you, I often wonder about the world I left."

Seraphina observed him with understanding. "You can always visit the shore, my love. You have the freedom to explore both worlds now. We can share every moment without losing any part of ourselves."

And so, under the canopy of stars, the couple

made a pact. Samuel would continue to journey to the shore, sharing the stories of the sea with the fishermen, while Seraphina would watch over the waters, ensuring their balance remained intact.

 Their love taught both land and sea the beauty of coexistence. Each day bloomed with vibrant life, eternally enriched by the kindred spirits who defied nature to unite.

      Years passed, and their love only deepened. As their love grew stronger, it unfurled into the universe's tapestry, reminding everyone that love knows no bounds or borders.

# THE ENCHANTED CIRCLE

In the heart of the mystical Eldenwood Forest, where ancient trees whispered secrets and moonlight danced upon the leaves, two powerful beings existed: a warlock named Thorne and a witch named Lyra. Thorne lived in a tall tower woven from ivy and stone, with a swirling mist that often obscured its base. He was a tall figure with tousled raven-black hair that framed his striking, angular features. His emerald-green eyes sparkled like emeralds in the light of the stars, and his presence commanded attention. The air was thick with magic, and a hint of danger accompanied him wherever he roamed.

Lyra, on the other hand, resided in a quaint cottage adorned with wildflowers and glowing crystals. With flowing auburn hair cascading down her back and hazel eyes that flickered with warmth, she radiated kindness and creativity. Her laughter echoed like windchimes, and her gentle spirit filled the air with a sense of peace. Lyra was known for her ability to heal; her hands glowed with a soft light when she tended to the sick or the wounded. Despite their disparate appearances and lifestyles, fate would bring their worlds together.

It all began during the annual Eldenwood Gathering, a magical festival that brought together beings of all kinds: fairies, elves, sprites, and magical creatures far and wide. The atmosphere was lively, filled with laughter and light, and the scent of blooming night flowers hung in the air. Thorne arrived at the gathering with his head held high, striding confidently through the throngs of revelers. His cloak billowed behind him, its deep blue hue somehow capturing the stars above.

As Thorne made his way through the crowd, he caught sight of Lyra, enchanting the onlookers with her skills. She gracefully moved her hands in a fluid motion, creating vibrant flowers that bloomed and danced around her. The spectators clapped in delight, their faces alight with wonder.

Thorn was captured. In that moment, the noise around him faded, and all he could see was Lyra. Time stopped and the festival faded, leaving them alone. He approached her, his heart racing in a way he had never experienced before. He felt a destiny-related familiarity with her.

"Your skills are remarkable," he said, his voice a deep, velvety tone that caught Lyra's attention. Her hazel eyes widened slightly as they locked onto his emerald gaze.

"Thank you," she replied, a blush creeping up her cheeks. "You're the famous warlock, Thorne. I've heard many stories about you."

"I hope they are good," he chuckled, a warm smile spreading across his face. His charm was intoxicating, igniting a spark of curiosity within her.

"Yes, they are," Lyra acknowledged, her own smile bursting. "However, some may perceive you as rather mysterious."

"Mysterious? Perhaps," he said, leaning closer. "But I assure you, I am not here to create fear."

And thus began their dance—a blend of conversation, laughter, and an unspoken connection that pulsed between them. They shared stories under the stars, spoke of dreams and spells, and reveled in the possibilities of their futures. The world around them seemed to disappear as the festival progressed, enveloping them in a bubble of enchantment.

The night was thick with magic, and as the moon reached its zenith, Thorne invited Lyra to witness the stars from his tower. It was a beautiful sight; the night sky was awash with shimmering constellations, each telling a story of its own. Lyra accepted, excitement fluttering in her heart.

They arrived at his tower and climbed to the roof. The air was cool, and the wind gently tousled their hair. Lyra gazed up, marveling at the vastness of the sky.

"Do you see that constellation?" Thorne pointed excitedly; his face illuminated with passion. "The Sorceress is the one over there." Legend says she represents the union of magic and love."

"Why do you know all this?" Lyra asked, her curiosity piqued.

"I spend many nights gazing at the stars, studying their secrets, much like you do with your plants," he replied softly. As he spoke, everything around them faded to gray, and the warmth that blossomed within their hearts shone brightly.

As their eyes locked, an unbreakable thread of understanding passed between them. In that instant, they both felt something indescribable —they were souls fated to intertwine. They shared their first tentative kiss under the blanket of starlight, the magic of the moment crackling like electricity in the air. It felt as if the universe had aligned perfectly for them, offering a taste of something magnificent yet fragile.

As days turned into weeks, Thorne, and Lyra's bond deepened. They met within the enchanting woods, where sunbeams pierced through the branches, creating a sanctuary just for them. They shared their knowledge about the mystical arts; Thorne taught Lyra spells of fire and air, while she revealed the secrets of healing and herbal magic to him. They balanced each other perfectly, each filling in the gaps of the other's abilities. Their laughter echoed through the trees, a melody that embraced the forest.

However, the world outside their magical bubble was not so kind. Whispers of discontent about their union began to cloud the woodland. The prideful factions of warlocks and witches viewed their partnership as unorthodox—a warlock and a witch together? They felt threatened by their wonderful connection, a partnership they had never heard of before.

One stormy night, while thunder rumbled and

lightning slashed through the sky, a council of warlocks convened to confront Thorne. Their eyes flickered with flames of condemnation; their faces lined with distrust. A stern, shadow-clad council leader spoke out against his relationship with Lyra, asserting that it would bring balance to their powers.

"Thorne, you are bringing shame upon our kind!" The leader bellows. "A warlock and a witch? This is madness! You could be so much more, yet you choose this path!"

Thorn's heart sank. He felt torn between his love for Lyra and the expectations of his kin. Ancient traditions bound him, demanding that he inherit the title of the strongest warlock, but all he could think about was Lyra's radiant smile. He stood firm, his voice steady. "I will not forsake my heart for tradition. Love knows no boundaries; not of magic nor of blood."

Yet the council would not relent. They concocted devious schemes to tear them apart, spreading rumors and casting spells meant to create discord between the two. Lyra, sensing the disturbance in the air, confronted Thorne one evening in their secluded grove.

"The air feels heavy, my love," she said, placing a hand on his arm. "I fear they are brewing trouble."

"I won't let them come between us, Lyra," Thorne vowed, but he could see the worry etched on her face. Storm clouds, dark and ominous, gathered above their grove, mirroring the turmoil within. "We'll find a way."

In the days that followed, they utilized their combined strengths to combat the wave of disapproval. Together, they created powerful charms to shield themselves from negativity, casting away the shadows that loomed over them. They wove spells filled with love and hope, crafting an unbreakable bond that even the fiercest storms could not tear apart.

Amidst all the chaos, they remained undeterred. Their love stood as a beacon of light, guiding them through the darkest nights. They learned to embrace the differences between them—a partnership forged not only in heart but in shared adversity.

However, the council didn't stop there; they initiated their ultimate attempt to undermine Lyra. With treachery in their hearts, they enchanted a creature of darkness—a Shadow Beast—sending it to attack Lyra while she was alone in the woods gathering herbs. As the beast emerged from the shadows, its eyes glowed like embers, and it moved with a grace that belied its ominous facade.

Lyra sensed the danger just as the creature lunged at her. Using her quick instincts, she conjured a protective shield of light that deflected the beast's strike. The light pulsated around her like a guardian, but she could feel her energy waning. Just as she summoned her strength, Thorne appeared, clad in determination.

"Lyra!" he shouted, rushing to her side. His heart raced as fear and adrenaline coursed through him.

With a firm resolve, he joined forces with her, their hands entwined. Together they unleashed their collective magic, weaving a tapestry of light and darkness that struck the very core of the beast. The creature staggered, feeling the combined force of their love—a love that shone brighter than any darkness.

In one final surge of power, they sent the Shadow Beast howling back to the depths from which it had risen. With its retreat, a sense of calm enveloped the forest once more. Exhausted yet exhilarated, Thorne and Lyra stood together, their hearts beating as one.

"We did it," Thorne breathed, pulling her close. "Our love conquered even the darkest forces."

"Yes, it did," she smiled, tears of relief streaming down her cheeks.

# LOVE WHISPERS FROM THE REALM UNSEEN

In a small town nestled between the mountains and the restless sea, an old mansion loomed over the landscape like a ghostly sentinel. Its ivy-clad walls and broken windows concealed secrets from decades past. Locals whispered tales of strange occurrences: dishes clattering in the dark, soft piano melodies drifting through the night, and glimpses of shadows flitting by late at night. For many, the old Holloway Mansion was a place of terror, but for Jenna and Ryan, it beckoned like a siren's song.

Jenna, with her fiery auburn hair and bright green eyes, had always felt a strong connection to the supernatural. She was a passionate paranormal investigator, skilled in using specialized equipment to uncover the ethereal threads connecting the living to the departed. Jenna's heart raced with excitement as she stood before the mansion's wrought-iron gates, its paint peeling and rusted, revealing glimpses of its former grandeur. "Tonight's the night," she said, her voice filled with determination.

Ryan, her partner in investigations and in life, stood beside her, his tall frame wrapped in a weathered leather jacket. He had soft brown eyes, filled with warmth, and dark curls that tumbled over his forehead. Ryan had always played the role of the skeptic, despite his unwavering support of Jenna's passion. "Are you sure about this place?

The last time we investigated, the spirit almost got aggressive." He chuckled, recalling their past adventure.

Yes, Ryan, these spirits are requesting assistance! They want their stories told. We owe it to them to figure out what's keeping them trapped here," Jenna insisted, her heart pounding not just from anticipation of the spirits within but also from something deeper—an invisible thread connecting her to Ryan.

As they stepped through the gates, a gentle breeze swept through the air, rustling the leaves, and sending a shiver down Jenna's spine. Shadows almost entirely engulfed the mansion's grand staircase, making it even more imposing up close. They passed through the darkness with their flashlights, their hearts beating together in the silence.

As they entered the foyer, they noticed how dust danced in the beams of their flashlights, creating a surreal atmosphere reminiscent of a dream. "This place feels... alive," Ryan whispered, breaking the stillness. Though he often masked his inclination toward the paranormal, he even felt the energy crackling around them.

The initial exploration revealed artifacts hidden beneath layers of dust, one of which was a piano standing proudly in a corner, an alien presence amidst the crumbling wallpaper. It was as if each creak of the floorboards sang a symphony of forgotten melodies that echoed through time. Sweeping her hand across the piano's surface, Jenna could almost hear notes ringing in her imagination —the laughter of children, waltzes from grand balls, and whispers of love long gone.

Suddenly, a low hum began to fill the air, swirling around Jenna and Ryan like a tangible mist. Jenna giggled nervously, while Ryan raised an eyebrow, sensing that they were in for a unique experience. "Do you hear that?" she asked, excitement sparking in her voice.

"Yeah, but it's probably just creaky old plumbing," he replied with a smirk, hoping to lighten the mood despite his heart racing with intrigue.

The sound grew, as if it originated from deeper within the house, guiding them to a wide door at the end of the hall. After a brief hesitation, Jenna pushed it open, revealing a ballroom that sparkled with ghostly light, illuminating an ethereal dance of apparitions swirling gracefully around each other. Jenna gasped, astonished.

"They're dancing," she breathed out, her gaze locked onto the wraith-like figures whose laughter and whispers drifted to them like scents of perfumes worn in another century.

Ryan stepped closer to Jenna, adrenaline igniting between them. Their connection, one forged through countless investigations, suddenly felt charged, as if the spirits themselves were playing matchmakers. Unbeknownst to them, one ghostly couple observed their interaction with fascination, urging the very air around them to play along.

Yet the couple in the ballroom had an agenda. They had lived in the mansion decades ago and, witnessing the bond between Jenna and Ryan, wished to offer their spiritual assistance. They remembered love and wanted others to embrace it. Each flickering candle and swell of music became a whisper urging Jenna and Ryan closer, binding their hearts in a way none of their earthly concerns could penetrate.

"Let's join them," Jenna whispered, her curiosity and longing overpowering any doubts. Ryan hesitated but felt a pull he couldn't quite identify. As they stepped further into the ballroom, the ambiance shifted, enveloping them in warmth. The music seemed to swell, resonating a rhythm that matched their beating hearts.

Soon, they found themselves caught in its enchanting flow, moving together with grace, communicating unspoken feelings. Ryan enveloped Jenna in his arms, the scent of her hair mixed with the sweet essence of the ghostly air around them. As the apparition couples twirled and glided across the floor, they encouraged their connection. In those brief, ethereal moments, they were both adrenaline-driven investigators and lost lovers entwined in a dance that had echoed through centuries.

"This is incredible," Jenna laughed, feeling both terrified and thrilled.

But as the night wore on, things began to shift. The spirits grew more insistent, their laughter mingling with sobering whispers. "She's the one," one ghostly voice seemed to echo in Ryan's mind, filling him with doubt and joy simultaneously. "Protect her. Love her."

Invisible hands drew them deeper into the joy and fear battling within them. Jenna turned to look into Ryan's eyes, and what she saw took her breath away—an untold potential, a spark of deep commitment. Ryan's heart raced; he could feel a veil lifting, revealing a connection with Jenna that transcended even their investigations.

In the glow of that haunted ballroom, something undeniable passed between them—a promise hidden within tangled whispers. Just then, the music began to fade, drawing their bodies back to reality.

"Maybe we should head back," Ryan suggested, his voice catching slightly. He could still feel the warmth of her skin against his palm, fluttering just beneath the surface of their every movement.

But Jenna grasped his hand tightly, looking daring and resolute. "Not yet. I need to know. There's something here that's stirring my heart—a love that goes beyond the shadows."

With those words, the spirits gleamed, the mansion creaking with acknowledgment. Jenna's heart thudded wildly, and before she could analyze anything, she pulled Ryan into another intimate dance.

They twirled, nimbly gliding as their laughter rose to meet the ghosts in a harmonious symphony. And in that moment—that eternal, unguarded moment—Ryan finally found the courage to embrace the truth that had been present all along. **

"Jenna," he whispered, breathless and fervent. "I think I'm falling in love with you."

Her eyes gleamed like emerald jewels, reflecting the flickering lights of the room. "Ryan—"

A flicker of movement caught her eye, and they turned to find the ghostly couple watching them approvingly. They grasped hands and smiled knowingly as if gifting them a blessing that transcended human understanding.

"Forget the evidence," Ryan murmured, drawing

Jenna closer. As they locked eyes amidst the dance, he leaned in and whispered, "I want to be with you... forever."

In that beat of eternity, the ghostly couple reached forward, the waltzing music swelling until it enveloped them completely. The sound melded with their hearts' promises, becoming one mournful love song alongside the house's history.

Jenna nodded teary-eyed as she spoke. "Yes, I feel it too. Let's embrace this love... before they fade."

And with that declaration, the shadows above them billowed; the ghostly couple drew nearer, wrapping their ephemeral arms around Jenna and Ryan, weaving them into a tapestry of shared history.

As the dance continued, a powerful energy surrounded them, pressing to unite two souls eternally intertwined—not just with each other, but with the very core of Holloway Mansion and its whispering past.

"Together," Ryan said softly, gripping Jenna's hands firmly. They could feel the spirits' comforting warmth solidifying their bond, weaving strands that transcended their mortal existence.

That night was not merely an investigation. It became a love story reborn, one that echoed through soft sighs and ages long gone, leading them into a future crafted by both heartbeat and haunted memory.

Hand in hand, Jenna and Ryan emerged from the mansion; their hearts forever changed. The magic that thrived within its walls and its longing spirits infused their lives with courage and a love that could bridge any divide. As the dawn broke, they knew that their next adventure had begun — a story not just of the paranormal but of profound love, together, always.

# THE FORGOTTEN ILLUSIONS

In a quaint little town there stood an old, crumbling theater that had once been the crown jewel of the community. This theater, with its faded red curtains and cracked stage, was now home to Vincent, a magician whose best days lay in the distant past. Once known for his dazzling performances and extraordinary illusions, Vincent had recently lost his spark, fading into the shadows of obscurity. He lived alone, surrounded by dusty props and tattered plays that told tales of sold-out shows and thunderous applause. Now, those echoes were a distant memory, replaced only by his loneliness.

Vincent often sat in the theater alone, recalling the golden days when he would pull rabbits from hats and make silks vanish before grateful audiences. The thought of performing tugged at his heart, but every time he tried to practice, he felt an overwhelming sense of despair. His hands, once so deft and precise, now trembled as he shuffled cards in front of a cracked mirror that reflected not the magician, he once was but a shadow of a man defeated by life.

One moonlit evening, as he prepared for another night of solitude, Vincent heard a mysterious whisper in the air, almost like a forgotten memory stirring to life. "Vincent," it called, a voice both soft and shimmering like starlight. He turned toward the stage, his heart racing. Could it be a figment of his weary imagination?

And with the softest of footfalls, a figure emerged from the shadows — a radiant woman clad in a flowing gown that shimmered like ethereal mist. Her long, dark hair flowed around her shoulders as she approached, her luminous blue eyes glistening with warmth and strength. "I am Bess Houdini," she said, her voice as soothing as a gentle breeze.

Vincent blinked in disbelief. He stood before Bess Houdini, the legendary illusionist Harry Houdini's wife! He remembered snippets of her story—the woman who supported Houdini throughout his life, the brilliant mind behind many of his most celebrated illusions. "But how...why are you here?" he stammered, captivated by her presence yet bewildered by her sudden arrival.

Bess smiled knowingly. "I have been watching you, Vincent. Your struggle, loss of magic, and loneliness were palpable. Your heart calls out for help, and I am here to guide you back to your true self."

Vincent's heart began to flutter as he absorbed her words. Here was a woman whose spirit still lingered, transcending the boundaries of time and space, and she had come to seek him out. "But I've lost my magic, Bess. I don't know if I can ever find it again," he confessed, his voice barely above a whisper.

"You have merely misplaced it," Bess replied softly, stepping further into the light. "Just as Houdini lost many things in his life, including the allure of his magic after he embraced the inevitability of death," Bess stepped further into the light. Yet he sought solace in the knowledge he compiled throughout his career—the book of spells and tricks that he left behind."

Vincent's eyes widened with realization. "The book of Houdini... I've heard whispers of it, but it remains a myth... He carried this secret with him to his grave.

"Yes, but not entirely," Bess replied, her eyes sparkling with conviction. "It is hidden, but I believe with your talent, we can find it together."

An electric surge rushed through Vincent's veins as Bess reached out, taking his hands in hers. "Let us begin this journey. Together."

From that night forward, Bess appeared nightly, guiding Vincent through the vast array of magic tricks and illusions. Under her watchful gaze, he began to piece together his confidence. He practiced tirelessly, her laughter echoing in the stillness of the theater as she encouraged him. Each evening felt like a new performance—him learning the art of magic once more, and her gentle presence igniting a long-dormant passion within him.

One fateful evening, as they sat beneath the stars on the theater roof, Vincent, his heart pounding with sudden courage, turned towards Bess. "You've given me back my magic, my passion. But I have to ask—why me?"

Bess gazed at him, the moonlight casting a silver glow on her delicate features. "Vincent, it is not just your magic that has touched me. It is your heart; it is the way you approach this art. Magic is about connection—not just between a magician and an audience, but between hearts. I have felt so alone since Harry's passing, yet with you, I feel... alive. There is something here" — she gestured between them — "something beautiful."

Vincent felt the warmth spread through him, and for the first time in many years, he felt an inexplicable connection—one that transcended the boundaries of life and death. Vincent felt a yearning for understanding and cherished it beyond mere companionship.

As the days turned into weeks, Vincent and Bess grew closer, sharing stories of laughter and heartache. She spoke fondly of Harry—of all his magic tricks, but also of his dreams and desires, his passion for life. Vincent shared his dreams, his writer's heart, and his longing to revive the magic that once flowed through his veins. It was through explorations of the past and hopes for the future that they fell madly in love—a love that felt ethereal yet grounding, as if they had always belonged to one another across the tides of time.

Months passed in a whirlwind of creativity, filling Vincent's heart with hope and enthusiasm he thought had vanished forever. Together, they grew strong—her presence fueling his inspiration, his artistry resurfacing in ways he had only dreamed of. Each evening Bess would descend, guiding him as they searched for Houdini's secret book —a metaphor for rediscovering the magic within himself.

One fateful night, after a particularly enchanting rehearsal, Bess looked somber. "Vincent," she said, her voice trembling slightly. "Despite my desire to stay here with you, the realms beyond bind me." I can only remain in your world for a limited time to help you find the book and regain your magic. Once I complete that task, I must depart.

Vincent's heart broke at the thought of losing her. "I can't do this without you. You've reignited my spirit, my passion, everything," he pleaded, grasping her hands tightly, not wanting to let go.

Bess smiled, her eyes glittering with unshed tears. "You are stronger than you think, Vincent. This journey aims to reconnect you with yourself, granting you ownership of the magic. But we must locate Houdini's book together to solidify your newfound magic."

Overwhelmed with determination, they dove back into the search, their excitement driving them both. Vincent's mind flooded with memories of old trunks in decaying attics and dusty basements, where fading scraps of paper and forgotten possessions preserved fragments of Houdini's essence. They delved into libraries, trawled through archives of forgotten letters, and scoured estate sales for anything resembling a hidden treasure.

Finally, a few weeks later, in the dim light of an old antique shop cluttered with trinkets and memories, Vincent felt something draw him to a musty, leather-bound book wedged between a set of encased doves—a book that glowed with magic just waiting to be unleashed.

"Is this it?" He whispered, hesitant but hopeful.

Bess moved closer, laying her hand softly on the book's spine. "Yes, this is it, the treasure trove of secrets," she breathed, her voice barely a whisper.

Vincent carefully picked it up, cradling it as if it were a newborn. As he opened its pages, golden sparks danced around them, illuminating the space, and whispering the secrets of magic long forgotten. With every page turned, Vincent regained pieces of himself he thought lost forever—the memories of who he was merging beautifully with the man he had become in Bess's presence.

All at once, the space around them buzzed

with infinite possibilities. The air crackled with excitement, and Vincent knew he could bring a new life to magic—his own interpretation, his own essence, flowing freely through every trick and illusion.

But as the cards fell into place, the reality of Bess's departure loomed over him. "Vincent," she said, her voice laced with a bittersweet melody, "it's time for me to return now. You've found your magic again. You can create, inspire, and revive the wonder that remains in people's hearts."

"No! You can't leave me now!" He cried; the book clutched tightly in his hands. "Not after everything you've done—I can't face the world without you."

Bess stepped closer, her eyes glistening with the beauty of love and longing. "You will never be alone, Vincent. Our connection cannot be severed. Carry me with you in every performance, in your heart. Remember the love we've built here, the enchantment we've shared. Magic will reside in you forever."

Vincent reached out, desperately grasping at the fleeting shadows of her figure. "Will I see you again?" he whispered, feeling the strange heaviness consuming his heart.

"There will always be a part of me watching over you. And I will forever be a piece of your magic," she said gently, her laughter echoing like a familiar refrain as she began to fade into the tapestry of time.

And in that moment, Vincent understood. True magic lay not in fancy tricks or illusions, but in love, in connection, and the ability to evoke wonder in the hearts of those around him.

# ABOUT THE AUTHOR

## Prof. Robert Stewart Ph.d

Prof. Robert Stewart is a retired clandestine operative who was recruited, while a student at U.C. Berkeley, into a special program for humans with special abilities. He holds a DSc in Astronomy from Berkeley, and an Honorary Doctorate in World Religions from Provident University in Delaware. His fields of expertise are Martial Arts, child extraction from cults, world religions, science, and the Occult. Musician was his deep cover or camouflage life.

Prof. Robert Stewart is a multi-instrumentalist (saxophones, piano, flute, drum, vocals, etc.), composer, and producer. His two major label albums ("The Force" and "In the Gutta") were for Quincy Jones and Qwest/Warner Bros. records. He is known for his unique – personal sound and remarkably inventive improvisations declares Los Angeles Times journalist Bill Kohlhaase, as the lead tenor saxophonist on the Pulitzer Prize winning "Blood on the Fields" by trumpeter Wynton Marsalis, and as the protegé of saxophonist Pharoah Sanders. Jazz critic Jason Ankeny declared Stewart to be one of the most impressive jazz saxophonists to emerge at the end of the 20th century. Drummer Billy Higgins refers to Stewart as "perhaps the most important young artist to come along in decades."

# BOOKS BY THIS AUTHOR

**Children's Guide For Life**

**Astronomy For Teenagers**

**Jesus: The Evidence**

**Buddhism For Begginers**

**Science And Cosmic Messengers**

**Islam & Jihad (Holy War) Explained**

**The Real Mind Of God: A Comparative Scriptural Analysis**

Gender: Issues And Solutions

50 Compositions Of Saxophonist Robert Stewart